P9-APS-498

Copyright © 2006 by North-South Books Inc.

All rights reserved. No part of this publication may be reproduced,
stored in a retrieval system, or transmitted, in any form or by any means, electronic, mechanical,
photocopying, recording, or otherwise, without prior written permission from the publisher.

This edition contains the following copyrighted works:
Little Polar Bear © 1987 by NordSüd Verlag AG, Zürich, Switzerland
English translation © 1987 by Hans de Beer

Ahoy There, Little Polar Bear © 1988 by NordSüd Verlag AG, Zürich, Switzerland
English translation © 1988 by North-South Books Inc.

Little Polar Bear Finds a Friend © 1990 by NordSüd Verlag AG, Zürich, Switzerland
English translation © 1990 by North-South Books Inc.

Little Polar Bear and the Brave Little Hare © 1992, 1998 by NordSüd Verlag AG,
Zürich, Switzerland
English translation © 1992, 1998 by North-South Books Inc.
Adapted from the easy-to-read edition of the same title.

Library of Congress Cataloging-in-Publication Data is available.
CIP catalogue records for these books are available from The British Library.

This 2006 edition created exclusively for Barnes & Noble, Inc., by arrangement with
North-South Books Inc., New York, NY.

Barnes & Noble, Inc.
122 Fifth Avenue
New York, NY 10011

ISBN: 978-0-7607-8721-2

(Trade Edition)

3 5 7 9 10 8 6 4 2

Printed in China

The Adventures of
Little Polar Bear

Written and Illustrated by
Hans de Beer

NorthSouth
BOOKS
New York

The adventure begins . . .

Little
Polar Bear

It was a big day for Lars. He was going with his father on his first hunting trip.

Lars was white all over, just like his father. In fact, at the North Pole where Lars lived everything was white because it was covered in ice and snow.

Lars's father showed him how to do all kinds of things: follow tracks, swim, and dive. He talked and talked and Lars listened silently, paying close attention. Once his father disappeared underwater and stayed so long Lars began to worry. But when his father finally reappeared, he had a big fish for supper.

When it was time to go to sleep Lars's father said, "Make a big pile of snow to protect yourself from the wind, like I do."

Lars was proud of his pile, but also very tired. He quickly fell asleep, just like his father.

But during the night the ice began to crack. The piece where Lars was lying broke off.

When Lars woke up it was morning. He was all alone in the middle of the sea. It was getting warmer and warmer and the piece of ice and Lars's pile of snow were getting smaller and smaller.

When the ice was almost completely melted Lars saw a big barrel drifting by. Luckily Lars was able to reach the barrel and climb on top of it.

Then a storm began to rage. As Lars clung to his bobbing barrel he missed his father and his pile of snow more and more.

After the storm Lars drifted on the sea for a long time. At last he saw land but could not see any snow or ice. Almost everything was green and the sun was very warm. Lars carefully slid off the barrel and stepped onto the beach.

The beach was hot and yellow. It burned Lars's paws. He ran to a river nearby. But just as he was about to plunge in, a very big, tan animal sprang out of the water.

"Booo!" it said.

Lars quickly ran to hide.

"I was only joking," called the big, tan animal. "I'm Henry the hippopotamus. Who are you and why are you so white?"

Lars didn't know the answer to the last question. "Where I come from, everything is white," he said.

He told Henry about his long journey and asked him how he could get back to his father.

Henry listened sympathetically, but he seemed confused. He wiggled his ears and squirmed and finally said, "The only one who can help you is Marcus the eagle. He has traveled all over the world. He will know where you come from and how you can get back there. But we'll have to cross the river, go through the jungle, and climb the mountains to reach him."

Lars was happy to go, but when he looked at the river he said, "The only problem is that I can't swim very well yet."

"No problem at all," said Henry and laughed. "Climb on my back. I won't sink."

Lars was astonished by all the things he saw in the jungle. Henry patiently explained everything. Lars especially liked the tall, brown stalks that Henry called trees. They were such fun to climb!

In one brown stalk sat a funny green animal, which suddenly turned white, just like Lars.

"It's a chameleon," Henry said. "It can change its color."

Lars thought that was a handy thing to be able to do.

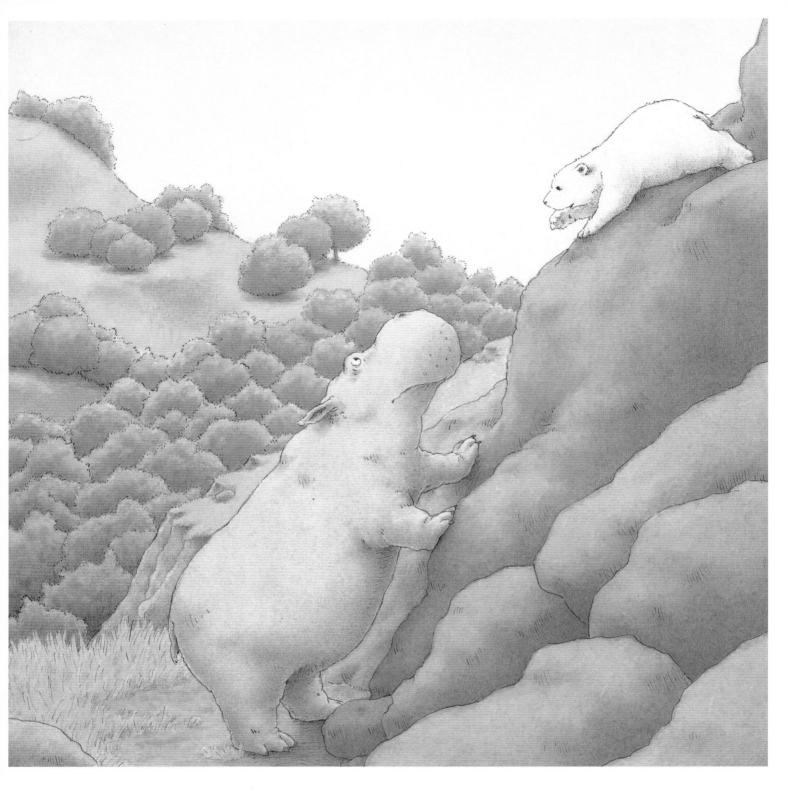

At the edge of the jungle, the mountains began. It was a bit cooler and Lars felt more comfortable. Henry found climbing difficult, but Lars helped by telling him where to step.

After a while Henry was exhausted.

"That's enough for today," he said. "Tomorrow we will continue. Let's rest here and look at the nice view."

As Lars looked out over the land and sea, he began to feel homesick.

"Cheer up," said Henry. "You'll be home again soon."

The next day they climbed higher. Henry had to stop often
to catch his breath. But at last he called, "Here comes Marcus!" as
a huge bird swooped down near Lars. Lars ducked.

"Don't be afraid," said Henry. "Marcus seems gruff, but he's
really quite friendly."

Henry said good morning to Marcus and politely explained why they had come.

The eagle looked at Lars and then said, "Well, well, a polar bear in the tropics! You're a long way from home aren't you, young man? Fortunately I can arrange your passage back. Tomorrow morning I will have Samson fetch you from the beach."

"Thank you very much, sir," said Lars shyly.

The next morning Henry and Lars met Marcus on the beach.

"Right on time," said Marcus proudly as a huge gray whale arrived.

Although Henry was happy for Lars, he was also sorry to see him go.
"Take care of yourself," he said sadly.

"Thanks for everything, Henry," Lars called as the whale swam away.
Marcus flew along a bit to set them on their way.

Henry stood alone on the beach. He kept watching for a long time after
Lars and the whale had disappeared.

Samson swam a long way until they were surrounded by ice and snow. "We must be near your home now," he said.

At the same moment Lars called, "There he is, my father! Father! I'm back!"

Lars's father couldn't believe his eyes. There was Lars riding on top of a whale.

Lars's father was very tired from looking for Lars. But he wasn't too tired to catch a big fish for Samson to thank him. Samson waved as he swam away.

"And now," said Lars's father, "we must go straight home because your mother is very worried."

On the way home Lars rode on his father's back. Everything was white and he was surrounded by snow and ice. But this time Lars talked and talked while his father was silent. He told his father about all the amazing things he had seen: Henry, the tall, brown stalks, Marcus, and much more.

"You didn't meet anyone who was white?" asked his father in surprise.

"Nobody, except a chameleon," said Lars, "but that doesn't count."

Lars had to laugh by himself because his father didn't understand his joke.

Ahoy There, Little Polar Bear

Lars, the little polar bear, lived with his mother and father near the North Pole where everything was white for as far as the eye could see.

Although he spent much of his time alone, he was happy.

But one day, when Lars swam quite far from his den, something terrible happened. Lars caught his foot, was pulled down deep into the sea, then yanked up in a gigantic net.

Lars was dropped to the ground with such a bang, he fainted. When he awoke he couldn't tell where he was. Above him was a ladder, so he climbed up the slippery rungs.

Lars roamed the long hallways. It seemed he was all alone until something rustled behind him. As he turned around two large eyes stared at him. Lars ran for his life.

Just when he thought he was safe again, he heard a voice, "Don't be afraid. It's only me, Nemo, the ship's cat. Welcome aboard."

Lars looked up. Above him was a friendly looking creature with orange fur. Lars could see that Nemo was an animal he could trust.

"I'm Lars," said the little polar bear. "I'm trying to get home as soon as I can."

"I'm afraid that isn't possible, at least not right away," Nemo said. "Your home is a long way from where we are now."

"Where are we?" asked Lars.

"We're on a ship, on our way back to port. Once we're there, I'll take you to see some friends who may be able to help. But until then there isn't anything we can do. Why don't we get something to eat? I expect you're very hungry."

When he had eaten, Lars felt much more cheerful. He curled up beside Nemo and fell fast asleep.

When they awoke, Nemo took Lars up to the deck. "Look," he said, pointing to the horizon, which was aglow with lights. "That's the port. We'll be there soon."

Lars was so excited he could hardly wait to go ashore. When the ship had come into port Lars eagerly followed Nemo onto the deck and over the plank.

"Try to look inconspicuous," said Nemo.

What Lars found on the other side of the plank surprised and disappointed him. Everything was so untidy and dirty.

"I'm afraid this isn't a very clean place," sighed Nemo. "We'd best hurry. Follow me around the back way. The streets are much too dangerous."

As Lars and Nemo made their way through alleys and back streets, Lars's white coat became dirtier and dirtier. He wished more than ever that he was home again, where everything was clean and white.

Following Nemo over fences and along walls took all Lars's efforts.

At last Nemo stopped. "We have arrived," he announced. "Wait here a moment."

It was very dark. Many eyes were staring at Lars. He grew quite nervous.

But the eyes belonged to some more cats who turned out to be just as friendly as Nemo.

The cats looked grave as Nemo explained Lars's problem. They thought it over for a few minutes. Then a black-and-white cat stepped forward. "I'm Johnny, also a ship's cat," he said. "My ship is leaving for the Arctic tomorrow. We must get you on board before daylight."

Lars, Johnny, and Nemo had to rush back through the alleys and backyards. Lars was so excited to be on his way home again, he forgot to watch where he was going and was almost hit by a truck.

When Lars reached the ship he said good-bye to Nemo quickly, for there was not much time. It was a sad moment.

For Lars, the time on the ship passed quickly. It wasn't long before he spotted something wonderful on the horizon. "Look, Johnny!" he shouted. "The North Pole. See how clean and white it is. I was once as clean and white as that."

That night, when the ship anchored, Lars thanked Johnny and set off for the beautiful white shores of the North Pole.

As Lars swam, the sea washed his fur clean. Once on shore, Lars ran for his den to greet his worried parents, who couldn't have been happier to see him. When Lars told his parents about his adventures, their mouths dropped open.

"And this is what Nemo looks like," Lars explained as he tried his best to look like a cat. Although his parents were not sure they understood, they were so happy to have Lars home again it didn't really matter. That night they all slept close together.

After that day, Lars's father often found his son gazing out at the horizon. "What are you looking for?" he asked.

"Ships," Lars said. "And cats, too. Some day a cat might fall off a ship and come to visit us."

Little Polar Bear
Finds a Friend

Lars, the little polar bear, was very lonely. As he gazed across the cool blue ocean he wished he had a friend to play with.

When he got home, Lars's mother could tell right away that something was wrong.

"Why are you so sad?" she asked.

"Because I have no friends here," said Lars glumly.

"Don't worry," said his mother. "One day you'll find someone to play with."

The next morning, when Lars went out for a walk, he thought he saw another little polar bear, standing next to a big wooden box.

"I should go over and say hello," thought Lars. But when he got closer he realized that the polar bear was made of wood.

Lars smelled food, so he walked into the box to see what it was. Suddenly there was a loud bang and the door on the end of the box snapped shut.

Lars was trapped!

It was so dark inside the box that Lars couldn't see a thing. He threw himself against the door, but it wouldn't open.

Lars sat in the box for hours. He thought about his parents and how worried they must have been when he didn't come home.

Suddenly he heard voices outside. The box began to move and Lars felt it being lifted.

He was very scared. The box bumped up and down and rocked back and forth for another hour. When it finally stopped moving Lars cried out, but no one opened the door.

Then the box began to shake and Lars heard a loud roar. He felt as if he was being pushed downwards and backwards, and there was a funny feeling in his tummy. Then the feeling passed. Lars was now very tired, so he curled up in the box and fell asleep.

The next thing Lars knew there was a loud crash, and at last the door to the box burst open. Lars found himself in a strange place, filled with many wooden boxes and lots of strange smells.

"Hey, little polar bear, come over here," said a deep, friendly voice. Lars looked up and was startled to see a huge walrus.

"What are you doing here?" asked Lars.

"I was trapped, just like you," said the walrus. "The owl says that we're being taken to a zoo."

"What's a zoo?" asked Lars.

"I don't know," grunted the walrus, "and I don't want to find out. Do you think you could lift the latch on this cage?"

Lars banged the latch with his paws and finally it swung open. The walrus lumbered out of his cage and together they started to free all the other animals.

As the cages were opened, Lars was surrounded by many animals he had never seen before. But the biggest surprise came out of the last box: a little brown bear whose name was Bea.

The walrus was very clever, and soon he had found a way to escape. But all the animals were so happy to be free that they ran away, leaving the slow walrus behind.

"Wait for me!" he cried after them.

When Lars and Bea heard the walrus cry, they stopped, turned around, and went back to help their friend. "I'm sorry we ran off," said Lars. "We started together and we'll finish together."

By the time the three of them reached the woods it was dark. They barely escaped being caught in the bright glare of searchlights. When they were deep in the woods and out of danger, Lars, Bea, and the walrus fell fast asleep.

The next morning when Lars woke up he was surprised to hear Bea crying.

"What's wrong?" asked Lars. "We're not in danger anymore."

"It's my parents," sobbed Bea. "They were captured earlier and I'll probably never see them again."

"I'm sorry," said Lars. But then he had an idea. "Why don't you come home with me!" he said happily. "You can be my sister."

"But won't your parents be upset because I'm brown?" asked Bea.

"Of course not," said Lars. "Bears are bears!"

When the walrus woke up, the three of them talked about how they would get home. "If we could find a river," said the walrus, "I could carry the two of you on my back."

While the walrus talked, Bea noticed some bees flying around a tree. "I'm hungry!" Bea said, turning to Lars. "Will you help me get some honey?"

Lars had never seen bees before and he was afraid. He hid behind some bushes with the walrus.

Lars and the walrus liked the honey very much, and as soon as they had eaten the three friends set off to find a river. As they walked along, Lars couldn't believe how many trees there were in the forest.

Luckily, Bea had such a good sense of smell that she quickly led them to a small stream. The walrus jumped right in and rolled around.

"This feels great," he said happily. "Climb on my back and let's get going!"

As the walrus swam along, the stream turned into a river. Lars told Bea all about his wonderful home.

Then Lars noticed a familiar smell. "We're coming to a city," he said. "I visited a city once. We must be very careful. Let's stop until it gets dark."

While the three of them sat on the riverbank and waited for the sun to go down, Lars told them about his adventure in the city. "I met some nice cats," he said, "but everything is very dirty. My home is much nicer than a city."

The next day, Lars and the walrus recognized the smell of salty seawater. "We're almost home," Lars said to Bea.

"Not quite," said the walrus. "We still have far to go. And first we have to pass through those big gates up ahead."

Soon they found themselves in the middle of the ocean. A storm had started and the waves were getting bigger and bigger.

"Hang on tight!" yelled the walrus.

At last, the three friends arrived in the Arctic. Bea stared at the strange landscape. She had seen snow before, but she had never seen so much of it.

The walrus dropped Lars and Bea off near Lars's home. It was time to say good-bye.

"Thanks for waiting for me," said the walrus. "I never would have made it home without you."

"And we never would have made it without you," said Lars.

As the walrus swam away, Lars and Bea set out to find Lars's parents. Bea was having trouble walking on the ice and snow. She kept slipping and sliding.

Suddenly Lars saw his parents and ran up to greet them. Bea slid along behind him.

"Where have you been?" said his mother. "We were so worried about you."

Lars quickly told his parents about his latest adventure and explained that Bea had been separated from her parents.

"She's afraid that you won't let her stay because she's brown," said Lars.

"That's silly," said Lars's father. "Bears are bears."

Lars's mother gave Bea a big hug. "You're a very beautiful bear," she said. "You can stay with us as long as you like."

Lars was very happy. "I can't wait to get home," he said. "There are so many things I want to show my new friend!"

Little Polar Bear
and the Brave Little Hare

Lars, the little polar bear, lived at the North Pole. He liked to sit on a little hill and look out over the ice and snow to the sea.

Usually it was very quiet at the North Pole; the only sound was the wind. But one day Lars heard something else, a faint whimper. He turned his nose in the direction of the sound and sniffed. He smelled something unfamiliar. On silent paws, Lars followed the smell until he found a deep hole. The whimpering clearly came from down in the hole. What could it be?

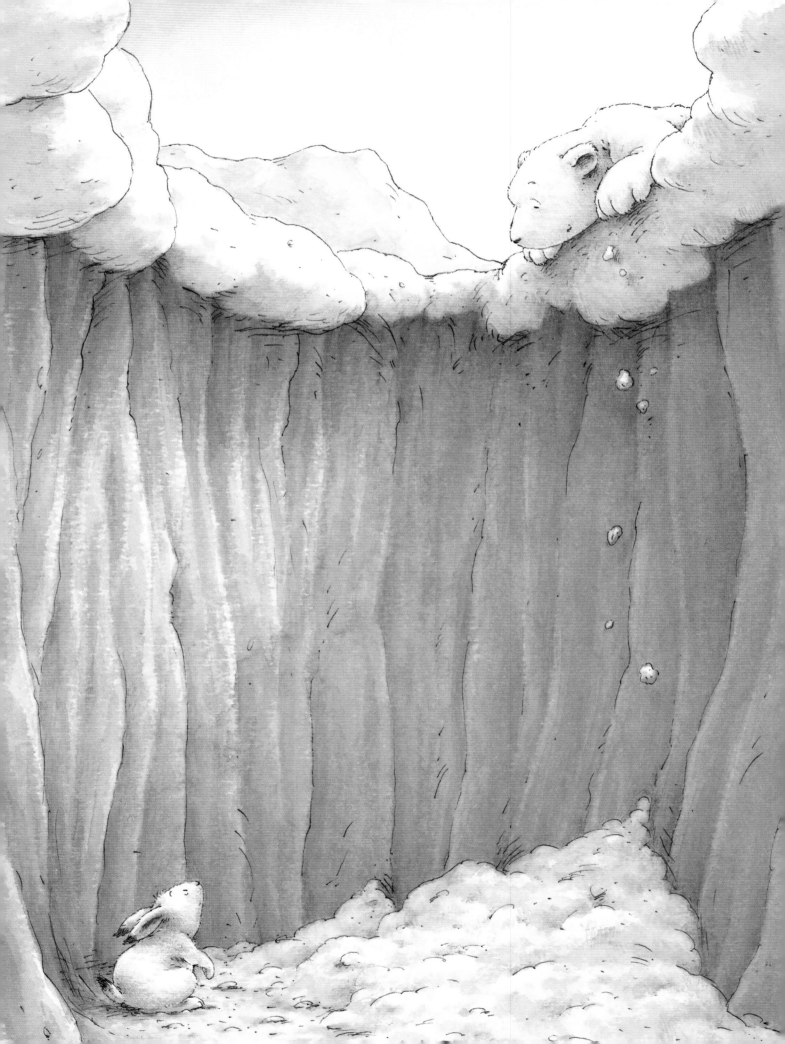

Lars leaned nervously over the edge. Down at the bottom sat a small hare, shivering with fear.

"Don't be afraid," Lars said to him. "I will help you."

The little hare's eyes grew large as Lars pushed down a heap of snow, but then he understood, and with a hop-hop-hop he was free!

"I was so scared!" said the little hare.

"Everything is all right now," said Lars. "What's your name?"

"I'm Hugo," said the hare.

"My name's Lars. Come on, let's race!"

"Great!" cried Hugo, for he loved to race. And he certainly could run fast, so fast that he easily beat the little polar bear!

Soon it started to snow.

"When it snows, I have to go home," said Hugo. "My parents said so."

That's too bad," said Lars. "But I'll walk you home."

It snowed harder and harder. The two struggled against the wind. The snow was so thick that they couldn't see a thing, so they snuggled up against each other and waited out the storm.

Finally it stopped snowing. The sky was bright and clear again. Lars and Hugo shook off all the snow. Everything looked different and strange.

"Where are we?" wailed Hugo. "We'll never find our way back home!"

"Don't worry, Hugo," said Lars. "I often get lost, but I always find my way home again."

"But I'm hungry," said Hugo.

Suddenly they heard a loud rattling noise. Something red was rumbling though the snow.

Hugo quickly burrowed into a pile of snow.

"You're such a scaredy-hare!" called Lars, laughing. "Come on out! That was only a car."

"A what?" asked Hugo from deep inside the snow.

"A car! It belongs to the polar station. My father takes me there all the time, and we find delicious things to eat! Come on! I know the way home from there."

Lars and Hugo followed the car's tracks. Soon they saw the polar station.

"Now that you know where we are," Hugo said, "let's go straight home!" The polar station made him nervous.

"Don't be a scaredy-hare," said Lars. "Let's get something to eat first."

"I'm not so hungry now," said Hugo.

"I am," said Lars. "Wait until you see what good things they have to eat down there. Come on!"

When the car left again, Hugo gathered his courage and followed Lars down to the polar station. In the rubbish behind the station they found fish, bread, and two crunchy carrots—enough for a little picnic.

"I'm just going to take a look around," called Lars to the hare.
"You can wait here if you want."

The little polar bear climbed up to the roof of the polar station.
He noticed an opening that wasn't a door and wasn't a window.
It had a funny smell. Lars heard an unusual noise. He wanted
to get a closer look, so he pushed aside the grate and leaned into
the opening. He still couldn't see, so he leaned in further and
further . . . and then . . . oops!

Lars fell headfirst into the shaft, but luckily he landed—PLOOF!—on a chair.

It was hot in the room. Everything bleeped and blinked in a frightening way. Now Lars wanted to go home, too! He looked around and noticed a door. Quickly he slipped through and looked for the way out. But all the doors to the outside were locked. Lars was really scared now.

Lars paced through the rooms. Suddenly he had a shock—the car was returning. Any moment now the man would be here! Terrified, Lars searched for a hiding place.

Hugo also heard the car. He saw the man get out. I have to help Lars! thought Hugo. His heart pounded wildly. Fast as lightning, he hopped down to the polar station. But the man was already at the door. What now?

With springing leaps, Hugo jumped up to the roof. He heard noises through the shaft. The man is down there! thought Hugo. I have to save Lars. But how?

Then Hugo got an idea. He turned around and pushed with his hind feet. Snow plopped down the shaft. He kept pushing, as fast as he could.

The man looked up. "What is happening on the roof?" he said, and headed out to see what was going on. He didn't notice the little polar bear, but he *did* leave the door open.

Lars slipped out the door, and as soon as he saw that the coast was clear, he ran away as fast as he could.

"Come down, Hugo, quick!" he called from a safe distance. "I'm out. I'm over here!"

Hugo dashed between the man's legs, and took one great leap off the roof.

Lars and Hugo ran and ran, as fast as they could. It was just like a race. And Hugo was still faster.

"Wait for me!" cried Lars, out of breath. Hugo stopped. They were already quite far from the polar station.

"I was so scared!" said Lars. "But you were very brave. You saved me. Now you can call me a scaredy-bear."

"I wasn't brave," said Hugo. "I just did what I had to do. And everything is all right now."

Together they found their way home.

Lars and Hugo became great friends. Often they would sit on the hill and look out over the ice and snow to the sea.
And sometimes they curled up together at night in the snow, whispering stories to each other until they fell asleep.